look for the
unicorn hiding
(you'll just see her horn)

Dear DAUGHTER
I LOVE YOU
because

You are more rare than a
meteor shower,

that explodes on the earth in a spray full of flowers.

You are more precious than a crystal mountain,

flowing with gemstones
in a sparkling fountain.

You are sweeter than a
donut sundae,

Covered in sprinkles and drizzled with honey.

You are braver than a
a kitten in space,

exploring the stars at a leisurely pace.

You are more magical than unicorns at play,

Dancing on clouds and singing all day.

You are cuter than a thousand puppies,

Rolling and laughing in a field full of bunnies.

You can be anything that
you dare to dream,

A scientist; a rock star, an astronaut queen!

You are more fun than fairies
at dawn,

Floating with butterflies
on a dew dusted lawn.

You are as special as a mermaid in motion,

With scales made of gold,
shining deep in the ocean.

You are more loved than all
the toys ever made,

When you're near
or you're far my
love will not fade.

You are talented, capable, confident and wise,

Cooler than llamas throwing a birthday surprise.

You are a beautiful girl, outside and in,

with sparkling eyes and a sweet little grin.

But there's a bigger reason I love you it's true,

It's because you are....

absolutely,

positively,

amazingly,

Made in the USA
Columbia, SC
06 November 2020